REMY AND RUBY'S RESCUE RANCH

Letting Go

By Katy Duffield

Illustrated by
Hazel Quintanilla

Rourke
Educational Media
rourkeeducationalmedia.com

A Division of
Carson Dellosa
Education

Dear Guardian/Educator,
Introduce your child to the wonderful world of reading with our leveled readers. Your growing reader will be continuously engaged as he or she is guided from one level to the next. Each level is carefully built to provide your child with the reading skills and knowledge to be a confident reader! Ultimately, we want your child to develop a love of reading.

Level 1 *Learning to Read*
High frequency words, basic sentences, large type, labels, full color illustrations to help young readers better comprehend the text

Level 2 *Beginning to Read Alone*
Short sentences, familiar words, simple plot, easy-to-read fonts

Level 3 *Reading on Your Own*
Short paragraphs, easy-to-follow plots, vocabulary is increasingly challenging, exciting stories

Level 4 *Proficient Reader*
Chapters, engaging stories, challenging vocabulary, multiple text features

Reading should be a pleasurable experience. A child who enjoys reading reads more, and a child who reads more becomes a better reader. Your child will grow with exposure to broad vocabulary and literary techniques, and will develop deeper critical thinking and comprehension skills. We are excited to be a part of your child's reading journey.

Happy reading,
Rourke Educational Media

www.rourkeeducationalmedia.com

Edited by: Kim Thompson
Cover layout and interior layout by: Kathy Walsh
Cover and interior illustrations by: Hazel Quintanilla

Library of Congress PCN Data

Letting Go / Katy Duffield
(Remy and Ruby's Rescue Ranch)
ISBN 978-1-73161-493-3 (hard cover)(alk. paper)
ISBN 978-1-73161-300-4 (soft cover)
ISBN 978-1-73161-598-5 (e-Book)
ISBN 978-1-73161-703-3 (ePub)
Library of Congress Control Number: 2019932403

Printed in the United States of America
01-0902313053

Table of Contents

Chapter One
A New Visitor

Ruby opens the barn door.

"Where are you, Auntie

Red?" Remy calls.

"Over here," Auntie Red says.

Auntie Red sits on a
stool. She holds something
wrapped in a towel. Remy
and Ruby move closer. A
feathery head peeks out.

"It is a barn owl," Auntie Red
tells them.

"Cool!" Remy says.

"Not cool!" Ruby says. She

points at the owl's sharp **claws**.

"Those are its talons,"
Auntie Red says. "Talons help
owls catch their food."

"This owl is the most
awesome thing I have ever
seen," Remy says.

Ruby keeps her distance. But

Remy reaches out to the bird.

"What's wrong with it?"

Remy asks.

"Its eye is hurt," Auntie

Red says.

Remy takes a closer look.

"Will it be okay?"

"I can't fix it. But it may heal
with time," Auntie Red says.
Remy frowns. "Poor owl."

Chapter Two
Holding On

Ruby is ready to do

something else. Remy isn't.

Ruby swings on the tire swing.

Remy stays with the owl.

Auntie Red and Ruby take a **hike**. Remy sings to the owl.

Ruby makes homemade

strawberry ice cream.

Remy strokes the owl's

smooth feathers.

Later, Auntie Red and Ruby
come back to the barn.

"I am sorry the owl is hurt,"
Ruby says.

"Me, too," Auntie Red says.

"But at least we get to keep him!" Remy says.

Auntie Red looks **puzzled**.

"I know you're attached to the owl," Auntie Red says. "But we need to let him go."

"But he can't see well," Ruby says.

"How will he **hunt** for food?" Remy asks.

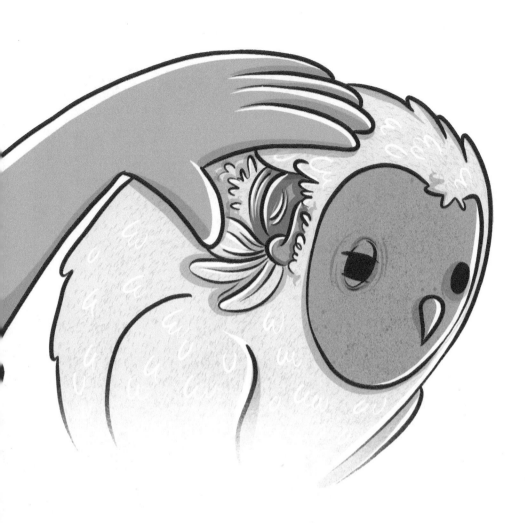

Auntie Red lifts the feathers

on the side of the owl's head.

"See his ears?" she asks.

Ruby and Remy nod.

"Barn owls mostly use their ears for hunting," Auntie Red says. "Their hearing is very strong. They can even hear a tiny lizard creeping across the ground."

Chapter Three
Letting Go

The next day, a warm
breeze blows through the
pines. Remy knows what day
it is. It is the day they will set
the owl free.

The family gathers at the
barn. Auntie Red brings out
the owl.

"Goodbye, owl," Ruby says.

"I hope you will come back

to see us," Remy says.

Remy strokes the owl's

feathers one last time.

Flap! Flap! Flap!

Ruby hugs Remy. Auntie Red holds his hand. They watch as the owl **soars** into the forest.

"It's sad to see him go,"
Ruby says.

"But at least we know he
will be okay," Remy says.

Remy, Ruby, and Auntie Red
are sad. But they know they
did the right thing.

"What can we do to cheer
us up?" Auntie Red asks.

"I have an idea," Ruby says.

"So do I!" Remy says. "Ice

cream!"

Bonus Stuff!

Glossary

claws (klawz): Hard, sharp nails on the foot of an animal or bird.

hike (hike): A long walk, often in the country or mountains.

hunt (huhnt): To chase and kill wild animals for food.

pines (pinez): Tall evergreen trees that have cones and leaves that look like needles.

puzzled (PUHZ-uhld): Confused or unsure.

soars (sorz): Flies or rises high in the air.

Discussion Questions

1. Why do you think Ruby was worried about the owl's talons?

2. Do you think letting the owl go was the right thing to do?

3. Do you think the story would have turned out differently if the owl's injury kept it from hunting?

Animal Facts: Barn Owls

1. Barn owls eat small animals such as mice, rats, frogs, and small birds.

2. One ear of the barn owl is higher on its head than the other. This helps the owl hear what's happening above or below it.

3. A barn owl's wings make very little noise when it flies.

4. Barn owls do not "hoot" like most owls. Instead, they make a screeching sound.

5. Barn owls usually hunt at night.

6. Wild barn owls eat about four small animals every night.

7. Barn owl feathers are super soft!

8. The barn owl's large eyes help it see well in the dark.

Creativity Corner

Imagine you have super-duper hearing like a barn owl. Write a story about what you might hear. What are good things about having strong hearing? What are bad things? Try to use at least three of the glossary words in your story.

About the Author

Katy Duffield is a writer who lives in Arkansas. She doesn't think she would like to hear as well as a barn owl because she is afraid all the little sounds she could hear would keep her awake all night!

About the Illustrator

Hazel Quintanilla loves her job, pajamas, burgers, sketch books, fluffy socks, and of course animals! Hazel had a ton of fun illustrating *Remy and Ruby's Rescue Ranch*.